MEET THE

Ryan Wilson

Age: 15

Secret Wish: that he went to public school so he could make friends his own age

Favorite Meal: sushi and a kale salad

Greatest Fear: not being recognized in public

Best Quality: super close with his little sister

CHARACTERS

David   NeD

the **OWENS** twins

Ages: 12

Ned's Hidden Talent: knows how to sew

David's Career Goal: open a farm-to-table restaurant in San Francisco

Family Fun: marathon games of Pictionary

Best Quality: respectful of their parents

1
THE CONTEST

Ned and David Owens were twins. They were both in sixth grade. They were not the kind of twins who looked alike. And for twins, they did not agree about much.

Ned
(2 minutes younger)

David
(2 inches shorter)

Ned liked to bowl. David liked to cook. Ned liked sailing. David liked to fish.

1

Ned liked classic rock. David liked hip-hop.

Ned's favorite   David's favorite

Sometimes they were buds. Other times, not so much.

There was one thing they both loved. It was a TV show called *Ryan's World*. They never missed it. It was the best.

The star was a kid in ninth grade. Ryan Wilson. He had won the Junior X-Games. He was great at extreme sports. He could break planks with his head. He sang. He played music. He was funny. And smart. Everyone loved him.

His show came on after dinner. One night the show was about a bully. Ryan put itch powder in the bully's bed. He said it was bedbugs. The bully ran out of his own room.

Ned and David loved the show. Their dad had once made them itch powder from rose hips. It was now in a box in the basement. He had put a little on the boys' arms. It worked great.

The last show ended with a live extra part. In it, Ryan talked about a big contest.

3

He would come to the winner's town. He would live with the winner for a week. He would even go to school with the winner.

It was like Ryan would be the winner's best friend. The week would be filmed. Then it would be shown as a special episode.

The twins begged their mom and dad.

"Can we enter?" Ned asked.

"Ryan can stay in the spare room," David told them.

"He can stay in our bedroom," Ned said. "It's bigger."

4

Their dad was doubtful. "Do we really want a TV crew here? In the house?"

"Yes!" Ned and David shouted at the same time.

"I don't see the harm. But don't think you'll win," Mrs. Owens warned the kids. "The odds aren't very good."

We have a better chance...

It was decided. They could enter. Ryan had explained the rules. Kids could enter by phone. He showed tables of helpers.

They would count calls. The five thousandth caller would be the winner.

"I'll take that call myself," Ryan said. He looked out from the TV screen. He was buff and blond. His smile was bright. "I can't wait to come to *your* town. We'll have a blast."

Ned smiled back at the screen. It was like Ryan was talking only to him.

Ryan counted down the time. "Okay. Start making your calls in five, four, three, two, one. Go!"

On your mark, get set, CALL!

Ned and David each had cell phones. They made call after call. Always busy. On the TV screen was the total number of calls. It rose fast.

"Getting close!" David shouted.

"You know it!" Ned said. "Just keep calling."

It was now or never. Ned called one last time.

2
WE WON!

It was so tense. Ned was not dumb. His mom was right. The odds were bad. But one thing was true. They would not win if they did not try.

"Five thousand." David saw the number on the screen. "Oh well. We lose."

Better luck next time

"It was a good try," Ned said. He had his phone to his ear. There were long beeps.

Like the call was ringing. The beeps went on. Ned was about to click off. Then he heard something.

"Ryan's World!"

The voice was male. It was one that Ned knew.

No. It couldn't be. But it was.

"Hi, I'm Ryan! Who've I got?"

Ned was so happy. He could barely say his own name. "I am N-n-n-ed. Ned Owens!"

He had crushed the odds. He had done it. He had won.

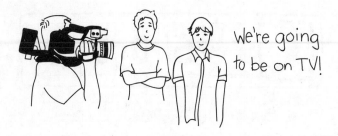

We're going to be on TV!

One week later, Ned and David were in the backyard. Their parents were there.

Also, a man named Mal Itkin. Mal was in charge of *Ryan's World*. He would also be in charge of Ryan's visit.

"Where will Ryan be sleeping?" Mal asked.

"We have an extra bedroom," said the twins' mom. "I'll make it up for him."

"Sounds great," Mal said. He turned to the boys. "Your job is to make sure Ryan is happy. Ryan's job is to make sure you're happy. It's going to be great."

Ned was so excited. He and David were already big stars. They lived in a small town. The whole town knew Ryan was coming. There was just one middle school. Everyone there wanted to meet the star.

"He's really going to hang out with us?" Ned asked.

"He'll do what you guys do!" Mal promised. "School, games, skating. Hanging out. Ryan is a real guy. A little older than you, but real. Really real. You know what I mean?"

Will Mom make Ryan finish his broccoli too?

Ned and David nodded. They knew it from the show. Ryan wasn't fake. He was *real*. That was why he was so great.

"Okay. He'll be here tomorrow. Right around two o'clock," Mal said. "Here's an idea. Plan a party for him."

Ned and David shared a fist bump. They would plan a party. It would be the best way to start the best week ever.

3
THE STAR

The party was ready. Ned and David had set it up with their buds. Tisha, Marie, and Paul were all fans too. They decided on a *Ryan's World* theme.

Tisha drew pictures of all the stars. On the show, Ryan loved burgers. It was his thing. The kids planned a backyard burgerfest. It would be kids and the camera crew. The adults would stay inside.

15

But Ryan was late. His plane from L.A. was delayed. There were delays with the limo. Then busy roads. The kids waited. The burgers got cold. The kids waited some more. But they were okay. They would wait forever.

Ryan will be worth the wait!

Ryan showed up three hours late. He was not as buff as he seemed on TV. He wore jeans and a Rolling Stones T-shirt. Ned and David went to greet him. Their friends were right behind.

Ned's heart beat like crazy. His favorite star was at his house. This was nuts.

Ned and David had made up a little speech for Ryan.

"Hi, Ryan," Ned said. "I'm Ned."

"And I'm David."

"We are so glad you're here. If we can do anything to make it more fun?"

"Just tell us!" David finished.

Ned stuck out his hand. Ryan shook it. He shook David's hand too. Then he met each and every kid. He posed for pictures. Ned thought that was so cool. He was so nice. When he was done, Ned asked him to join the party.

David waved to Marie. She turned on an old Rolling Stones song. Ned grinned. Marie had to have seen Ryan's T-shirt. She was smart.

Ryan took Ned aside after the cameras stopped filming. "Um, dude? I'm not big on parties."

"Excuse me?"

No more party? We didn't even get to the burger eating contest!

The star put an arm around Ned. "Like I said, Neddy boy. I'm not big on parties."

Ned was surprised. "But Mal said to plan a party."

18

"I get it. I do," Ryan said. "But he didn't talk to me about it. I mean, in Hollywood? It's party, party, party. I'm partied out. I don't need one more. I've had a big day. Long time to get here. You get me?"

Ned flushed. Of course Ryan would not want a party. He had to be tired after his big trip.

"I get you," Ned said. "How about if we just hang? Like, for an hour? Then I can tell everyone to go home. You can get some rest."

Ryan's arm stayed around Ned. "I don't need rest, Neddy boy. I need to do something else. Hey. You got a bowling alley in this town?"

Bowling
beats burgers

Ned nodded. "Sure. Bowl-A-Lot Lanes. Over on Main Street."

"Great!" Ryan punched the air. "Bowl-A-Lot Lanes it is. How about we go bowl a lot? Right now!"

4
GUTTER BALL

"Hey! That's Ryan Wilson!"

"Yo, Ryan! Over here!"

"Can I get a kiss?"

"Can I get a hug and a kiss?"

"Can I get a hug and a kiss too? Ooh, and a pic?"

I guess he's used to this.

It had not taken more than ten seconds. Ned had opened the door to Bowl-A-Lot. Ryan had strutted inside. The camera crew was already there. Ryan got mobbed on his first step.

Ned and David stood off to one side. All they could do was watch. Their parents were there too. Also Mal Itkin.

"Sorry about the party thing," Mal told them. He rubbed his own head. "I know it was a lot of work."

We all had to get up early...
ON A SUNDAY!

6:00

"Don't worry about it," Mrs. Owens said. She was being a kind host. She had worked hard on the party. They all had. Everything had been set. But Ryan had nixed it. Well, it was their job to make Ryan happy. That was what Mal had said.

"Check him out," David said. Ryan was with a bunch of teen girls. All the cameras were on him.

Does he ever take those sunglasses off?

"He seems good here," Ned commented.

"I guess," David said.

"Go bowl," Mal told the kids. "The show will pay. Games, shoes, food. Bowl all the games you want."

"Is Ryan going to bowl?" Ned asked. "I'd love for him to bowl with us."

"Sure, sure," Mal said. "I'll send him right over."

Do we really have to wear those?

All the kids got bowling shoes. They were sent to lanes nine and ten. Ned was a good bowler. But he bowled badly. He kept hoping Ryan would come over. He didn't.

Ryan just went from lane to lane. He took pics with kids and adults alike. He joked around. He seemed to be having fun.

"He should be with us. Do I go say something to him?" Ned asked his brother.

David shook his head. "Nah. Take it easy. We have a whole week."

That was true. They did have a whole week. Ned tried to focus on the game. But he still rolled a gutter ball in the last frame. It gave him a score of 67. That was the lowest he had bowled in years. That was when Ryan came over.

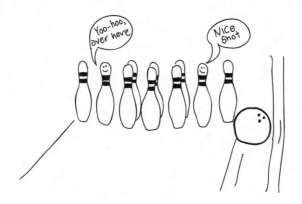

"How'd you do, Neddy boy?" Ryan asked. He checked out the score. "Wow. Sixty-seven? That's all you got?"

Ned felt bad. He wanted Ryan to see that

he could do better. Then Ryan saw more girls wave to him. He took off to say hello.

"I thought he wanted to bowl," Ned said sadly.

David shook his head. "Know what? For Ryan Wilson, this *is* bowling."

5
SUPERTEXTER!

The camera crew and Mal followed Ryan, Ned, and David. They headed for the spare room. Ryan gave a play-by-play as he walked.

"So this is the Owenses' place," he told the crew. It was like the twins were not even there. "It's a real small town. I'm going to have a real small-town guest bedroom. And here I am!"

The invisible Owens twins!

He led the crew into the spare room. It was simple. A bed. A desk. A dresser. One window. A green rug. Bare walls.

Ryan cracked up. "This is not like my crib in L.A. That's for sure!"

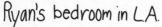

Ryan's bedroom in L.A.

Pacific Ocean!

"Tell us if you need anything," Ned offered.

"Yeah. Totally," David told him.

Ryan sat on the bed. "How about a beer? And some pizza flown in from New York."

Ned and David shared a look. Was he really asking for—

"Come on. Neddy boy. You guys!" Ryan laughed the laugh the boys knew from his show. "I'm joking. You know? A joke?"

Ryan turned to the crew. "Look. It's been a long day. How about you guys call it? Let me hang with the boys for a few."

Finally. Ryan wanted to hang with them. This was just what Ned had been waiting for. A chance to get to know Ryan.

Ned had so many things he wanted to ask. Did Ryan like to skate the most? Or snowboard? Would he ever do MMA? Could he show Ned a bike trick later in the week?

← That would be awesome!

The crew filed out. Ryan's word was law.

"I can get us some drinks. And chips," David offered.

Ryan nodded. "That sounds great. I'll be right here."

Then the star's phone sounded. He dug it out of his jeans. It was the latest Apple model.

"Stand by, guys. I gotta deal with this text."

Ryan's thumbs went nuts. Ned had seen fast texters. But Ryan was faster than fast. He was like Supertexter.

"I'll get the chips," David said. He left. Ned and Ryan were alone. Ned watched Ryan text.

Finally, Ryan finished. He grinned at Ned. The phone was still in his hands.

"Sorry about that. Work. You know. So, Neddy boy. Tell me about you."

Ned grinned. His moment had come. He had been waiting a long time. "Well, I'm just your basic kid. I'm in sixth—"

Ryan's cell sounded again. He checked it. A phone call this time.

"Sorry, Neddy boy," he told Ned. "Gotta take this. It's the Coast. You know. West Coast. Hollywood. My lawyer."

INCOMING CALL:
HOLLYWOOD

Ryan swiped his finger. "Hey, man. How are you? I'm doing that small-town thing. You know. We talked about it. It's *wild*."

David came back with a tray of drinks and chips. Ryan stayed on the call. He mostly listened. Finally, Ryan put the phone aside.

Sour Cream + Onion
Ryan's favorite

"Sorry, guys." He shook his head at the boys. "This is big. A movie deal. A big movie deal. Maybe we can do this another time. How about in the morning?"

"We have school," Ned told him. "We *all* have school."

Ned was sad. But Ryan was a star. If someone wanted him in a movie, they would call him. It was normal. "You're coming. Right?"

Ryan grinned. "Wouldn't miss it. See you guys later."

Ned and David left the room.

"That was not fun," David said.

"Not fun at all," Ned agreed. "Like bowling. And the party we didn't have."

The next day would be school. A new day. A fresh start. Ned looked forward to it. It had to be better than the first day had been.

33

6
SCHOOL DAZE

"Our school is so lucky to have him here today. What a day! What a gift! Let's hear it for the star of *Ryan's World*. Ryan Wilson!"

Principal Kwan waved to Ryan. Ryan came across the stage. The whole school was in the gym. Six hundred kids shouted. Ned and David sat in front. Everyone knew Ryan was living with them.

Sick of all the screams for Ryan

35

A girl asked Ned to save Ryan's hair from the shower. Ned did not tell her the truth. That he'd barely said ten words to Ryan. The star was always doing one of two things. He was on his phone. Or he was talking to his fans. It was one or the other.

Mrs. Owens had asked him that morning about food. Did he want to eat? Ryan was too busy texting to answer. It was rude.

Ryan came to the mic to talk. The kids roared. Mr. Kwan finally held up his hands. That got the gym quiet. It took about a minute.

"Thanks, thanks," Ryan said. "It's so great to be here. I love you guys!"

The kids cheered louder. Ned looked around the gym. Every face was shining.

"First thing I want to do is thank my hosts. Ned Owens? David Owens? You guys are the best. Stand up. Get some love! Give it up for Ned and David!"

The crowd cheered louder than ever. Ned and David sat between Marie and Paul. Their friends made them stand up. Ryan ran down to be with them. The crowd went wild. Even Mr. Kwan took some cell phone pics.

The assembly was all about Ryan. He talked about his career. He told jokes. He showed clips from the show. He broke bricks with his fists. He did skateboard tricks. He even put himself down. He called himself lucky. "I'm so lucky to be on TV. I bet there's a kid at this school who is as good an actor as me. Go for your dreams. I will cheer for you the whole way."

Ryan showing off

The kids cried with joy. Teachers loved it. Mr. Kwan told everyone to listen to Ryan. Finally, it was time to go back to class. Ryan was to go with Ned to math. Then he would go with David to PE. And then with Ned to English. But he came to the boys shaking his head.

"Can't do class," Ryan told them. "Big meeting later."

Ned was surprised. He wanted to be a good host. But this was so sudden.

"Meeting?" Ned asked. "How come? You just found this out?"

Ryan tapped his phone. "Phone meeting. Came up like that." He snapped his fingers. "That's showbiz. Anyway, I'll catch up with you later. Hm, where is Mal? Oh, here he comes."

And just like that, Ryan ditches us. AGAIN!

Mal came over. "Ryan told you about his meeting?"

Ned nodded.

"It's big," Mal said.

"What's it about?" David asked.

"His career. What else?" Mal said.

"What time is it?" Ned pressed. "Can't he just come to one or two class—"

Mal cut him off. "Come on, Ryan. Time is not on our side. We're out of here."

They walked down the hall.

Ned looked at David.

David rolled his eyes. "Whatever."

"You think he really has a meeting?" Ned asked.

David shrugged. "If you ask me? He hates math."

7
THE MEETING

That night, Ned and David ate at Smith's Diner. It was the best place in town. Their parents took them. Mr. Smith had run it for forty years. Ned had asked Ryan to come and meet Mr. Smith. Ryan said no. He had to work out. Then he would eat with Mal.

Ryan's dinner

Our dinner

Ryan did not even say sorry. The family went to dinner alone.

The boys got burgers. Their parents got salads. They sat in silence until the food came. Then Mr. Owens spoke. "This isn't what you wanted, is it, boys?"

"The burger? It's just what I ordered. The rest of the week? Not so much." Ned tried not to sound bitter.

His brother drank some root beer. "I think Ryan is a jerk. He just does what he wants. He's always on his phone."

"I think that's true of a lot of kids," Mrs. Owens told them.

"Sure. But the boys have a point," Mr. Owens said. "Ryan is treating them badly."

"You can say that again." Ned ticked off the points on his fingers. "Want to know how? Here's the list. He bails on the party.

He ignores us at home. He's always texting. He ditches us at school. And it's only Tuesday."

Ready for Ryan to go

← We'll even help you pack!

David nodded. "And he's here until the end of the week."

Mrs. Owens added some dressing to her salad. "Okay, then."

Ned raised his eyebrows. "Okay? Now what?"

Mrs. Owens looked right at him. "Okay, then. You boys have said what you think. Now you need to man up. You are hosts.

43

Hosts are kind to their guests. I think Doctor Seuss said that."

Mr. Owens nodded. "I agree with your mother."

"You always agree with Mom!" David accused.

"That's because I'm smart." Mr. Owens smiled. "But she's right. You are the hosts. Your job is to be good at it."

"He's here for just a few more days. Deal with it." Mrs. Owens ate some lettuce.

The boys knew when a talk was over. And this talk was over. They had been told to put up with Ryan. No matter what he did. No matter how he acted. No matter how much it hurt.

8
PARTY!

Ned and David tried to be kind to their guest. Ryan did not make it easy.

The next day the big star skipped school again. The boys stayed strong. They went to school. When kids asked about Ryan, they said he was busy. Mr. and Mrs. Owens went to work. It was a day like any other.

Where's Ryan?

Still, Ned felt empty. The week was such a bust. The funny thing was how no one else was mad at Ryan. Other kids were just glad he had come to town.

"Don't be down," Marie told him. "Ryan's a big star. He's doing star things."

Marie still
LOVES Ryan

After school, Ned and David walked home. They got close to their house. There was a lot of noise coming from the back.

"You think Ryan is back there?" David asked.

Ned nodded. "Could be."

They walked around the side of the house to the backyard. What they saw made them gasp. There was a party going on. And what a party it was. There was a deejay. Someone had put up a hot tub. Teens were in it. The boys did not know any of them.

Someone had dug a fire pit. Chefs were cooking. There were tables, chairs, and even dancing. The star of the show was Ryan. The cameras followed him wherever he went.

Who are all these people?!

Oh no! Mom's garden is ruined!

"Mom won't be happy," Ned muttered.

David could not believe his eyes. "You can say that again."

"He said he didn't like parties!" Ned told David.

"Maybe he changed his mind," David said.

Ned waved to Ryan. Ryan saw him. He grinned and came over to talk.

"Hey! David! Neddy boy! Join the party!"

"Do my parents know about this?" Ned demanded.

"Nope."

"Who are all these people?" David asked.

"Buds from L.A. The TV show flew them in. Just for the party."

For a party? We've never even been on a plane!

"You can't do this," Ned said. "You can't have a party in our backyard. You can't dig a hole. Or bring in a hot tub! You didn't even ask our parents. Where's Mal?"

"He went to the store," Ryan said. "Relax, dude. We'll wrap by five. It'll be clean by six. They get home at what time? Six thirty? They won't even know it happened. Look. I need this party for the TV show. Relax, Neddy boy. Come on and have fun. Want me to hook you up with some girls?"

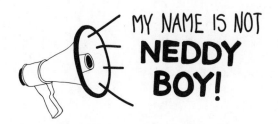

MY NAME IS NOT **NEDDY BOY!**

"No," David said. What was Ryan thinking? "We do not want you to hook us up with girls. We're in sixth grade!"

Ryan shrugged. "Well. I asked. Take it easy. Hey. You can say you partied with Ryan Wilson."

Ned fumed. He knew he should be kind to his guest. But Ryan said he wasn't big on parties. And now this? Was it all a lie? It was too much.

He did not want to think about what Ryan would do next.

9
PAYBACK

"It's only two more days," Mrs. Owens said. "Maybe we can wait."

"No. I've had it up to here." Mr. Owens touched his head. "There is a limit. I am at it. That crazy party? It was too much." He turned to his sons. "What do you boys want to do?"

David jerked his thumb at the front door. "Get him out of here."

Strike 3.
He's out of here!

Mrs. Owens looked at Ned. "How about you?"

Ned gave it a moment. He had really wanted to win the contest. He had been Ryan's biggest fan. Then he saw who the big star was in real life. It was hard to take.

"I'm ready for him to go. But I also want him to learn a lesson. That you get what you deserve. I think I know a great way to do it."

"What's that?" David asked.

Ned's grin got bigger. "Well, I learned it from Ryan's show."

You're going down, Ryan!

He whispered in David's ear. David's eyes got big. "I love it!"

"What are you boys thinking?" asked Mr. Owens.

Ned shared his idea. His father and mother both laughed.

"It's very funny. I approve," his dad said. "What about you, Val?"

Mrs. Owens had a twinkle in her eye. "Well, you know I don't care for payback. But I think this is fine. No one gets hurt. And I'm sure he'll want to sleep somewhere else."

Ned felt great. They had a plan. Now he and David had work to do.

The itch powder was still in the basement. The boys tried it on their arms. It still worked. All it took to make the itch go away

55

was cold water. They got it ready. They also got some black pepper.

Ryan was not home. He had gone with Mal to the next town over to meet more kids. The camera crew was gone too. The kids went into his room. They pulled back the sheets on his bed. They put itch powder down by where his legs would be.

After that, they made his bed just like before. Their parents let them stay up until Ryan got home. That was at about ten o'clock.

"Hey, guys!" Ryan came into their room. "Up late?"

"Homework," Ned fibbed.

"A lot," David agreed. "You're lucky you didn't come to school with us."

"How was the night?" Ned asked.

"Great! Met a ton of fans. It was cool." Ryan yawned. "I'm tired. I'm going to bed."

"Us too," Ned told him. "Tons of tests in the morning."

Ryan went to his room. Ned and David tried not to laugh. He was in for a big surprise.

He has no idea!

They turned out the lights and waited. And waited. And waited.

"What's he doing?" Ned hissed.

"Texting, I bet."

"Well, he needs to get in bed—"

"DANG IT! WHAT'S GOING ON?"

The cry had come from Ryan's room.

Yes!

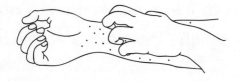

"What's going on?! My entire body itches!"

Ned and David grabbed the pepper. They ran down to Ryan's room. Ryan was in gym shorts. He sat on the chair. He was clawing at his legs. "Killer itch! What the heck? What's wrong with my bed?!"

"Don't know," Ned told him. "Let's see."

The boys went to the bed. The covers were pulled back. David put a little pepper on the sheets. Ned pointed to it.

"Bedbugs"

"Sorry, man," Ned said. "Bad news. I think you have bedbugs. You must have brought them in with you. Yuck."

He hoped Ryan did not think of the *Ryan's World* episode with the bedbugs.

Ryan didn't.

"Bedbugs! Ew! Lemme see!"

Ryan came to the bed. Ned pointed to the pepper specks. "See? Those are bugs."

"Get me out of here!" Ryan found his

phone. He scratched his legs even more. Then he called Mal. He told Mal to check him into a hotel. He didn't care where.

In ten minutes, Ryan was out the door. It could have been faster. But he had stopped a bunch of times to scratch.

10
A NEW CONTEST

A big group of kids was in the living room. Marie, Paul, and Tisha were on the couch. Other kids were on the floor. They had all come to watch *Ryan's World*. It would be the show about the visit with Ned and David. It was called "Ryan Wilson Goes Small Town!"

Grab some popcorn. It's almost showtime!

"Quiet!" Ned shouted. The show was about to start. He could not wait to see it. The guy had been such a jerk. Ned and David no longer liked Ryan. None of their friends did either. But Ryan was still a big star. He had signed up to do a movie. It would be out next summer.

no way we're seeing that

The show started. Every time Ned and David were on the screen, the kids cheered. There was film of the welcome. The bowling.

The school gym. Even the backyard party. Sometimes Ryan talked. He spoke about his love for the town and the school. He spoke well of the boys' parents. He saved the best for Ned and David.

"These are two great guys," he said. "It's not easy to have me as a guest. I'm so busy. Plans change so much. And they were the best. Ned? David? If you're out there? I love you guys!"

David + Ned got a RAVE review!

"★★★★★"

— Ryan

There was cheering for this too. Ned didn't care. He kept waiting to see the bad sides of the visit. How Ryan was on his

63

phone all the time. How he was rude. How he set up a party without asking. How he never went to class.

There was none of it. Not even once. Not a single word about bedbugs.

As he was leaving town, they had told Ryan about the itch powder. He did not get mad. He said it was funny.

There was a break before the last part. Ned turned to his dad. "It's so fake! I was there. You were too. It was not like that at all."

His father smiled. "Welcome to TV. A lot can change when it gets made."

"You can make a bad thing seem like a good thing?" Ned asked.

"And turn a good thing into a bad thing," his mom added. "That's why I like books."

"But he's not telling the truth!" Ned said.

Mr. Owens smiled. "Ned? TV isn't the truth. It's TV."

Reality   ⟶   Reality TV

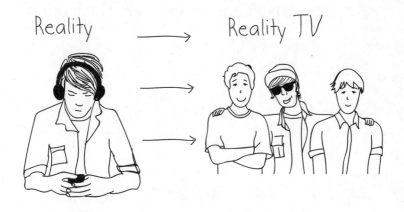

"Shush!" Marie got them to be quiet.

Ryan was back on the screen. He said

the visit with Ned and David had been so great. He was ready to do it with another kid. In another town. Maybe even the same town. They would do the same call-in thing to enter.

Everyone hooted at this.

"Anyone here want to enter?" Mrs. Owens asked.

The kids in the living room all said the same thing. Ned and David were the loudest of all.

"NO WAY!"

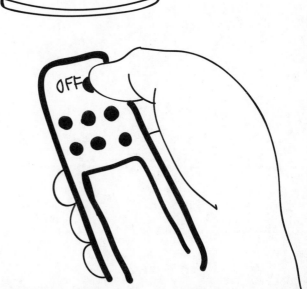